'strad
A465
Ebbw Valley
NANTYGLO ROUNDHOUSE
TREDEGAR
Afon Lwyd Valley
EBBW VALE
Coity Mountain
Rhymney Valley
Sirhowy Valley
ABERTILLERY
A4042
PONTYPOOL
NAL
BARGOED
BLACKWOOD
TREHARRIS
CWMBRAN
A449
Cwmcarn Forest
Twmbarlwn
OD
M4
M4
D BRIDGE
CAERPHILLY CASTLE
NEWPORT
CAERPHILLY
TREDEGAR HOUSE
Craig yr Allt
M4
Garth Hill
A48
CARDIFF
A48
Key
Castle
Mine
Iron Works
Roman Fort

HOMETOWN HISTORY
WELSH VALLEYS

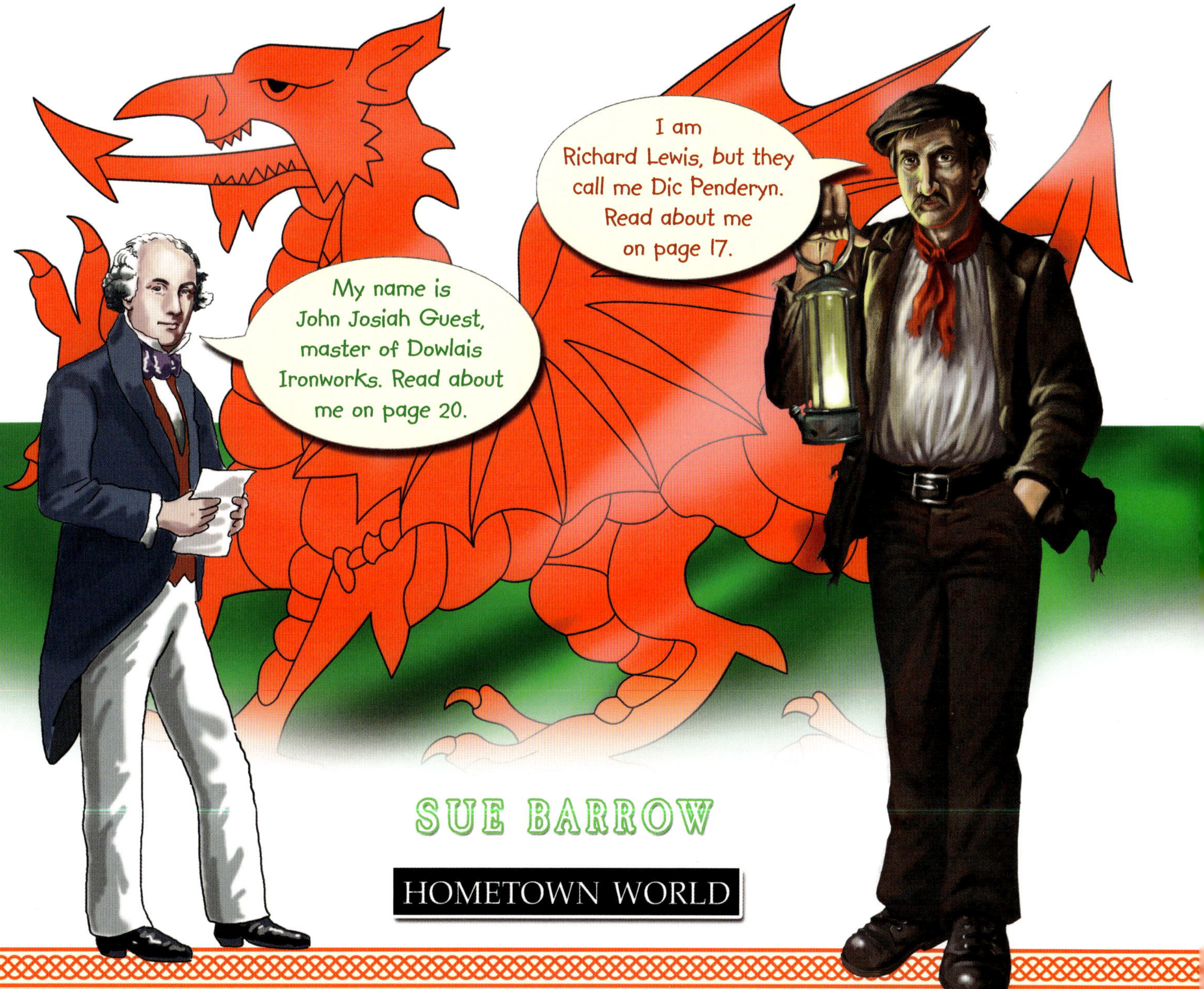

SUE BARROW

HOMETOWN WORLD

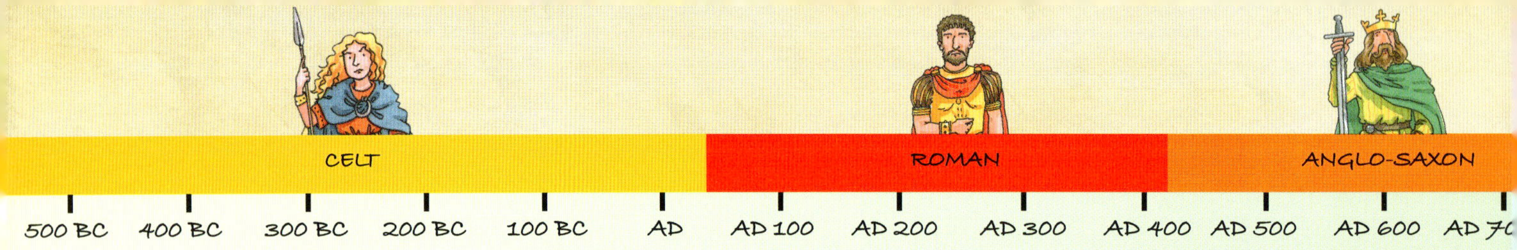

How well do you know your town?

Have you ever wondered what it would have been like living in the Valleys in Roman times? What about rubbing shoulders with the Iron Masters? This book will uncover the important and exciting things that happened near your home town or village.

Want to hear the other good bits? You will love this book! Some rather brainy folk have worked on it to make sure it's fun and informative. So what are you waiting for? Peel back the pages and be amazed at what happened in the Valleys near your home.

THE FACTS

Timeline shows which period (dates and people) each spread is talking about

CELT 500 BC | ROMAN AD 43-410 | ANGLO-SAXON AD 450-1066 | VIKING AD 865-1066 | MEDIEVAL TIMES 1066-1485 | TUDOR 1485-1603 | STUART 1603-1714 | GEORGIAN 1714-1837 | VICTORIAN 1837-1901 | MODERN TIMES 1902-NOW

The Roman Forts

The centurion raises his standard. Soldiers clatter behind him, their shields heavy after a day's marching from the fort at Gelligaer. They come to a halt and a gust of wind stirs the legion's flag. Along the straight road ahead the centurion can just make out the outline of Isca Silurum. Closing his eyes he pictures the hot baths awaiting them. He gives the signal to move on. They will be home by nightfall.

Excavations in the 20th century revealed the size and layout of the fort at Caerleon.

Plan of Isca Silurum

Barracks
Workshops
Headquarters
Hospital
Fortress Baths
Amphitheatre
Baths

Isca Silurum

When the Romans first arrived in Wales around AD 50 they had to fight against the local Celtic tribe, the Silures, led by Caradoc. They set about building a fort at Caerleon. It was a good place to build because it was close to the sea and well-protected. Launching an attack meant scrambling up the high mud banks of the river and then across a 10-metre deep ditch. The Romans used oak logs as foundations for the ditch and these were still in place when the site was excavated nearly 2,000 years later.

The fort, called Isca Silurum, was the headquarters of 6,000 highly-trained troops of the 2nd Legion Augusta. It was huge, about the size of 25 football pitches!

This marble stone, probably from the south west gate, shows the inscription 'Legio II Aug', an abbreviation for 2nd Legion Augusta.

Life Inside the Fort

Inside the fort, there was a granary for bread-making along with workshops, stores and a hospital. Caerleon even had its own kiln for making pottery.

Just outside the fort there was a large bath-house with an exercise hall and swimming pool to keep the soldiers clean and fit! There was also a large amphitheatre where fighting displays and other types of entertainment were put on.

The fort was called Isca Silurum after the river Usk and the land around it.

There were separate entrances and bathing times for men and women at the baths.

Auxiliary Forts

To secure the area, the Romans built a network of smaller forts across the Valleys, with Roman roads to link them. These forts probably had cohorts of about 500 soldiers guarding them.

The fort at Caerphilly might have been uncovered earlier if the 13th century castle hadn't been built on top of it! This site may have been chosen because it was on the road to the lead mining site at nearby Machen. It also had clear views of the Rhymney Valley and paths up Caerphilly Mountain. This gave the Romans plenty of warning of raids by the Silures.

The fort at Gelligaer was smallest but still impressive. It had arched gateways and a double roadway with guard towers on either side.

To the north, the fort at Penydarren overlooked the River Taff. Local people kept it supplied with beef and grain. Even oysters were brought in from the coast. Remains of the fort were discovered underneath the football ground where Merthyr Tydfil Football Club now plays.

My sandals aren't much use in this Silurean weather.

SPOT THIS!
This bread was stamped using a die with the words 'Century of Quintinius Aquila'. The bread would have been made for the 80 soldiers led by centurion Quintinius Aquila. Can you spot the die at the National Roman Legion Museum at Caerleon?

4 ...AD 50 ROMANS ARRIVE IN WALES...AD 75 ISCA SILURUM HEADQUARTERS...

...AD 90 AMPHITHEATRE BUILT...AD 380 ROMANS BEGIN TO LEAVE... 5

Clear informative text

Hometown facts to amaze you!

'Spot this!' game with hints on something to find in your area

THE EVIDENCE

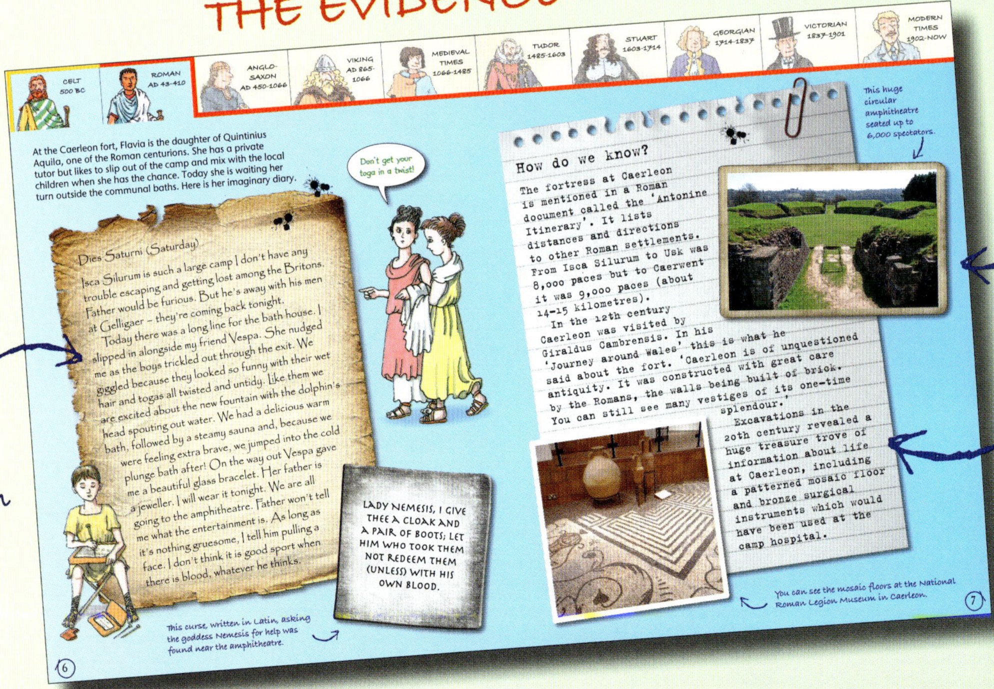
CELT 500 BC | ROMAN AD 43-410 | ANGLO-SAXON AD 450-1066 | VIKING AD 865-1066 | MEDIEVAL TIMES 1066-1485 | TUDOR 1485-1603 | STUART 1603-1714 | GEORGIAN 1714-1837 | VICTORIAN 1837-1901 | MODERN TIMES 1902-NOW

At the Caerleon fort, Flavia is the daughter of Quintinius Aquila, one of the Roman centurions. She has a private tutor but likes to slip out of the camp and mix with the local children when she has the chance. Today she is waiting her turn outside the communal baths. Here is her imaginary diary.

Dies Saturni (Saturday)

Isca Silurum is such a large camp I don't have any trouble escaping and getting lost among the Britons. Father would be furious. But he's away with his men at Gelligaer – they're coming back tonight.

Today there was a long line for the bath house. I slipped in alongside my friend Vespa. She nudged me as the boys trickled out through the exit. We giggled because they looked so funny with their wet hair and togas all twisted and untidy. Like them we are excited about the new fountain with the dolphin's head spouting out water. We had a delicious warm bath, followed by a steamy sauna and, because we were feeling extra brave, we jumped into the cold plunge bath after! On the way out Vespa gave me a beautiful glass bracelet. Her father is a jeweller. I will wear it tonight. We are all going to the amphitheatre. Father won't tell me what the entertainment is. As long as it's nothing gruesome, I tell him pulling a face. I don't think it is good sport when there is blood, whatever he thinks.

Don't get your toga in a twist!

LADY NEMESIS, I GIVE THEE A CLOAK AND A PAIR OF BOOTS; LET HIM WHO TOOK THEM NOT REDEEM THEM (UNLESS) WITH HIS OWN BLOOD.

This curse, written in Latin, asking the goddess Nemesis for help was found near the amphitheatre.

How do we know?

The fortress at Caerleon is mentioned in a Roman document called the 'Antonine Itinerary'. It lists distances and directions to other Roman settlements. From Isca Silurum to Usk was 8,000 paces but to Caerwent it was 9,000 paces (about 14–15 kilometres).

In the 12th century Caerleon was visited by Giraldus Cambrensis. In his 'Journey around Wales' this is what he said about the fort. 'Caerleon is of unquestioned antiquity. It was constructed with great care by the Romans, the walls being built of brick. You can still see many vestiges of its one-time splendour.'

Excavations in the 20th century revealed a huge treasure trove of information about life at Caerleon, including a patterned mosaic floor and bronze surgical instruments which would have been used at the camp hospital.

This huge circular amphitheatre seated up to 6,000 spectators.

You can see the mosaic floors at the National Roman Legion Museum in Caerleon.

6

7

Go back in time to read what it was like for children growing up in the valleys

Intriguing photos

Each period in the book ends with a summary explaining how we know about the past

VIKING
MEDIEVAL TIMES
TUDOR
STUART
GEORGIAN
VICTORIAN
MODERN TIMES
800
AD 900
1000
1100
1200
1300
1400
1500
1600
1700
1800
1900
2000

Contents

The Roman Forts

The centurion raises his standard. Soldiers clatter behind him, their shields heavy after a day's marching from the fort at Gelligaer. They come to a halt and a gust of wind stirs the legion's flag. Along the straight road ahead the centurion can just make out the outline of Isca Silurum. Closing his eyes he pictures the hot baths awaiting them. He gives the signal to move on. They will be home by nightfall.

Excavations in the 20th century revealed the size and layout of the fort at Caerleon.

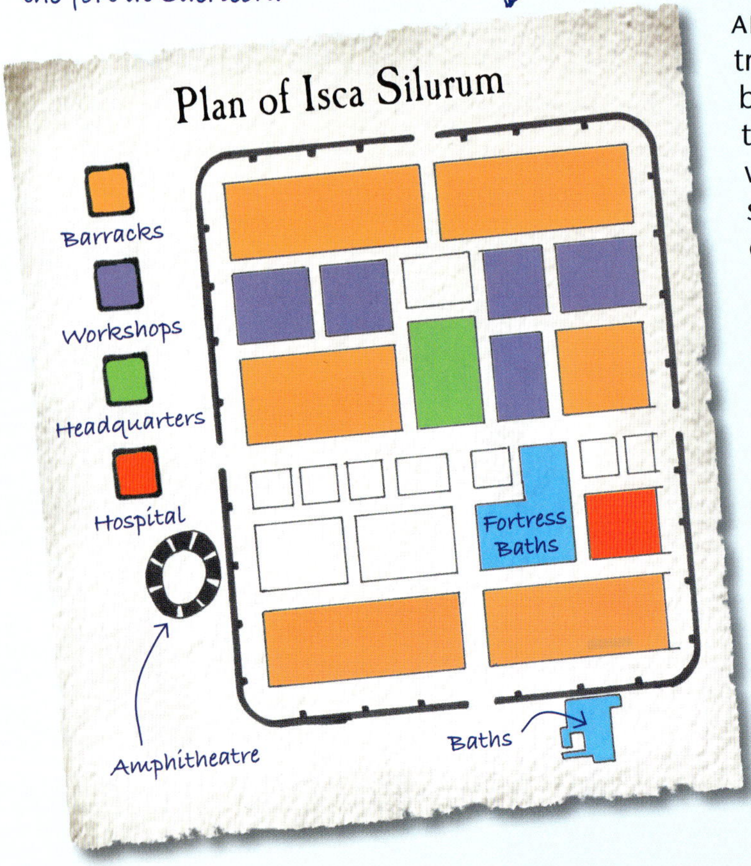

Isca Silurum

When the Romans first arrived in Wales around AD 50 they had to fight against the local Celtic tribe, the Silures, led by Caradoc. They set about building a fort at Caerleon. It was a good place to build because it was close to the sea and well-protected. Launching an attack meant scrambling up the high mud banks of the river and then across a 10-metre deep ditch. The Romans used oak logs as foundations for the ditch and these were still in place when the site was excavated nearly 2,000 years later.

The fort, called Isca Silurum, was the headquarters of 6,000 highly-trained troops of the 2nd Legion Augusta. It was huge, about the size of 25 football pitches!

This marble stone, probably from the south west gate, shows the inscription 'Legio II Aug', an abbreviation for 2nd Legion Augusta.

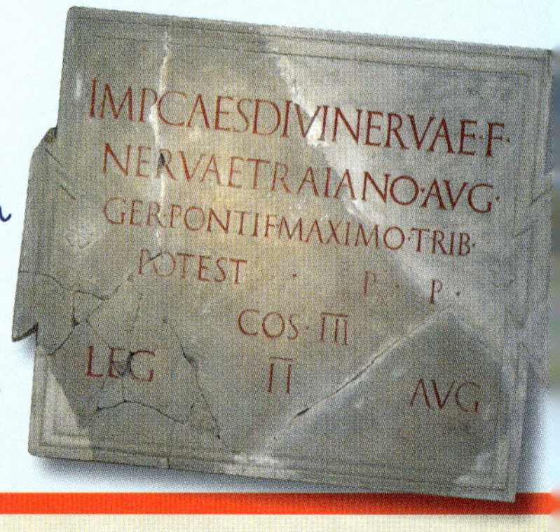

Life Inside the Fort

Inside the fort, there was a granary for bread-making along with workshops, stores and a hospital. Caerleon even had its own kiln for making pottery.

Just outside the fort there was a large bath-house with an exercise hall and swimming pool to keep the soldiers clean and fit! There was also a large amphitheatre where fighting displays and other types of entertainment were put on.

There were separate entrances and bathing times for men and women at the baths.

The fort was called Isca Silurum after the river Usk and the land around it.

Auxiliary Forts

To secure the area, the Romans built a network of smaller forts across the Valleys, with Roman roads to link them. These forts probably had cohorts of about 500 soldiers guarding them.

The fort at Caerphilly might have been uncovered earlier if the 13th century castle hadn't been built on top of it! This site may have been chosen because it was on the road to the lead mining site at nearby Machen. It also had clear views of the Rhymney Valley and paths up Caerphilly Mountain. This gave the Romans plenty of warning of raids by the Silures.

The fort at Gelligaer was smallest but still impressive. It had arched gateways and a double roadway with guard towers on either side.

To the north, the fort at Penydarren overlooked the River Taff. Local people kept it supplied with beef and grain. Even oysters were brought in from the coast. Remains of the fort were discovered underneath the football ground where Merthyr Tydfil Football Club now plays.

SPOT THIS!

This bread was stamped using a die with the words 'Century of Quintinius Aquila'. The bread would have been made for the 80 soldiers led by centurion Quintinius Aquila. Can you spot the die at the National Roman Legion Museum at Caerleon?

At the Caerleon fort, Flavia is the daughter of Quintinius Aquila, one of the Roman centurions. She has a private tutor but likes to slip out of the camp and mix with the local children when she has the chance. Today she is waiting her turn outside the communal baths. Here is her imaginary diary.

Dies Saturni (Saturday)

Isca Silurum is such a large camp I don't have any trouble escaping and getting lost among the Britons. Father would be furious. But he's away with his men at Gelligaer – they're coming back tonight.

Today there was a long line for the bath house. I slipped in alongside my friend Vespa. She nudged me as the boys trickled out through the exit. We giggled because they looked so funny with their wet hair and togas all twisted and untidy. Like them we are excited about the new fountain with the dolphin's head spouting out water. We had a delicious warm bath, followed by a steamy sauna and, because we were feeling extra brave, we jumped into the cold plunge bath after! On the way out Vespa gave me a beautiful glass bracelet. Her father is a jeweller. I will wear it tonight. We are all going to the amphitheatre. Father won't tell me what the entertainment is. As long as it's nothing gruesome, I tell him, pulling a face. I don't think it is good sport when there is blood, whatever he thinks.

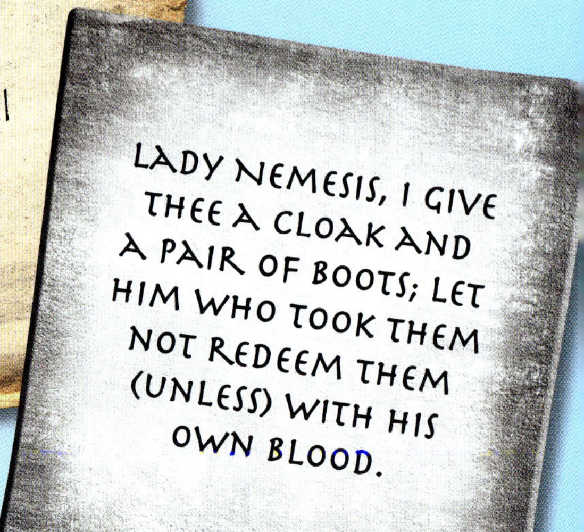

This curse, written in Latin, asking the goddess Nemesis for help, was found near the amphitheatre.

How do we know?

The fortress at Caerleon is mentioned in a Roman document called the 'Antonine Itinerary'. It lists distances and directions to other Roman settlements. From Isca Silurum to Usk was 8,000 paces but to Caerwent it was 9,000 paces (about 14-15 kilometres).

In the 12th century Caerleon was visited by Giraldus Cambrensis. In his 'Journey around Wales' this is what he said about the fort. 'Caerleon is of unquestioned antiquity. It was constructed with great care by the Romans, the walls being built of brick. You can still see many vestiges of its one-time splendour.'

Excavations in the 20th century revealed a huge treasure trove of information about life at Caerleon, including a patterned mosaic floor and bronze surgical instruments which would have been used at the camp hospital.

This huge circular amphitheatre seated up to 6,000 spectators.

You can see the mosaic floors at the National Roman Legion Museum in Caerleon.

Mountain Dwellers

There's a storm coming! **The travellers trudging up the bleak mountainside turn for a moment. In the valley below rain hangs like a thick grey curtain. Thunder crashes, lightning flashes. The men wave wooden crooks at their livestock to move them on. The women bend into the wind, clutching the hands of the little ones.** ***Hurry, hurry! We must find shelter.*** **Another flash and they spy a dwelling. A long house. A figure peers out from the entrance.** ***Come inside. Plenty of room for you and your animals.***

Early Settlements

When the Romans left Britain in about AD 410, the Celtic people of the Valleys were left to themselves. They were farmers, breeding sheep, cattle and pigs. They probably lived in isolated hillside farms. There were no towns or markets so people grew their own food and made their own clothes. Their homes were little more than small round huts. Later they built long rectangular dwellings, made of wattle (wooden branches) and daub (clay).

Some people lived in platform houses. The 'platform' was made by digging into the side of the mountain and piling the earth downhill. In better-quality houses a gutter around the back provided drainage. In the poorest houses the roof simply rested on the bank.

It was usual for people to share their homes with their livestock, with the animals at one end of the hut. Animals provided much-needed warmth in the winter.

For the next 500 years, warlike raiders called Anglo-Saxons came by sea from Germany, Denmark and Holland. The Anglo-Saxon invaders were pagans who believed in war as a way of gaining land and slaves. But there is no record that they landed in any part of Glamorgan or came to the Valleys from the north.

...AD 410 ROMANS FINALLY LEAVE BRITAIN...AD 480 TYDFIL IS KILLED...

Tydfil the Martyr – Fact or Fiction?

From the 5th century, Christian monks, who were later called 'Saints', sailed between Wales and Ireland converting pagans to Christianity. An Irish prince, Brychan, who became King of Breconshire, is said to have had 50 children by three wives! One of his daughters, Tydfil, was converted to Christianity as a young girl. In about AD 480, Tydfil was travelling to Hafod Tanglwyst farm in Aberfan, when she was attacked by pagans and killed. Tydfil was thought of as a martyr for her faith. The town of Merthyr Tydfil (which means 'the burial place of Tydfil') is named after her.

This window in Llandaff Cathedral shows the martyrdom of Tydfil.

How do we know?

The journey of the 5th century Irish monks can be traced by a series of large stones called the Ogham Stones. They have lines and markings on the edge recording the names of travellers in ancient Irish and sometimes Latin. One of these stones sits in the front porch of St John's Parish Church in Cefn Coed, Merthyr.

Records of Brychan and his large family were not written until about AD 1100 so they may not be reliable. Some people think that the story of St Tydfil is just a local legend. But there are local place names and churches around Merthyr Tydfil which point to a connection with Brychan's children.

SPOT THIS!

This Ogham Stone stands in front porch of St John's Parish Church in Cefn Coed, Merthyr. How many markings can you find on it?

St Tydfil's Church was eventually built on the site where Tydfil is thought to be buried.

Conquests and Castles

The wind is whistling. The dogs are howling. There is much fear in the Norman castle in Caerphilly tonight. Messengers bring news that Llywelyn and his men have been sighted over the Beacons. With torches of fire they are burning their way to victory. Gilbert the Red is abroad fighting religious wars. Will he return in time to avoid disaster or will Llywelyn capture the castle? But as the sky lights up red in the distance they are preparing for the worst.

The Welsh Princes

When the Normans arrived after 1070 they began to take control of the lowlands of Morganwg, the Welsh kingdom north of Cardiff. But the mountainous part, Senghenydd, was defended by the Welsh lords in their castles. Castell Meredydd was built on the ridge above the Machen Gorge. This was an important position because it linked the conquered lowlands with the Welsh uplands. Further north, Ynysycrug Castle in Trealaw, was built close to what is now Tonypandy town centre. And Castell Nos stood on the hills above Maerdy to defend the Rhondda Fach.

Gilbert de Clare

In about 1270 the powerful Norman Lord of Glamorgan, Gilbert de Clare, rebuilt Castell Coch in Tongwynlais on the ruins of Ifor Bach's castle. He also built Morlais Castle above Merthyr. He was known as Gilbert the Red because of the fiery colour of his hair. As part of his plan to conquer the surrounding uplands, he captured Gruffydd ap Rhys, Lord of Senghenydd, and had him imprisoned in Cardiff.

Llywelyn the Last

Gilbert de Clare soon faced a new enemy who was just as ambitious – Llywelyn the Last, Prince of Wales. Llywelyn controlled most of north and mid-Wales. But in 1266 Gilbert de Clare seized Senghenydd and began to build a castle in Caerphilly. The castle was built using wooden scaffolding. Before Gilbert could finish it Llywelyn attacked in 1269 and burnt it to the ground. But Gilbert carried on building a massive stone fort that was impossible to capture. When Caerphilly Castle was completed it was considered to be the strongest in Britain. Llywelyn was finally killed in an ambush in 1282 and beheaded.

Soldiers attacking Caerphilly Castle would have to find their way past a moat, a drawbridge and a portcullis to get into the outer part of the castle.

Caerphilly Castle is the second largest castle in Britain.

Llywelyn the Last was declared a rebel by the English King, Edward I, in 1276.

SPOT THIS!

Can you spot this statue of Llywelyn the Last? Clue: look inside Cardiff City Hall.

Llywelyn Bren

Llywelyn Bren was Lord of Senghenydd and under the authority of Gilbert de Clare. When de Clare died in battle, Payne de Turberville, who lived in Coity Castle near Bridgend, took control of his estates, taking land from Bren and others. Llywelyn started a revolt against the overlord on 28th January 1316 by attacking Caerphilly Castle. Bren and his men captured the constable, killed some of his men and burnt the town to the ground, but they couldn't capture the castle. Bren was finally defeated and he and his family were imprisoned in the Tower of London. Llywelyn was tried at Cardiff Castle and condemned to death. In 1318 he was hanged, drawn and quartered. He is buried in Grey Friars, Cardiff.

Will Rolfe is a local boy working in Gilbert the Red's household. He is only 13, but the stable marshal has put him in charge of feeding and grooming Gilbert's horse. Will is worried. He has heard the gossip in the stables – he knows there are troubled times ahead. Here is his imaginary letter.

It was when I was grooming Lord Gilbert's horse, Merlin, that I heard them talking about the Welsh prince, Llywelyn. They're right to be afraid of him and his mighty army. The labourers have only just started rebuilding at Caerphilly after Llywelyn and his knights burnt the last castle to the ground. What a terrible night that was. Fire and smoke enough to choke us all to death. It was a miracle we got the horses out. In the meantime we are billeted at Castell Coch. His lordship's personal servants are quite comfortable, sleeping on floors strewn with rushes and herbs to make them smell good. But my master, the stable marshal, laughs and says we are better off bedding down with the horses and livestock. We can disappear into the woods if the castle is attacked. They say Caerphilly Castle will be a mighty fortress when it is finished, well supplied with food and with a proper garrison of soldiers. Blacksmiths to shoe the horses and coopers to make the ale casks. Not like this place, high on a hill and miles from anywhere.

Plan of Caerphilly Castle

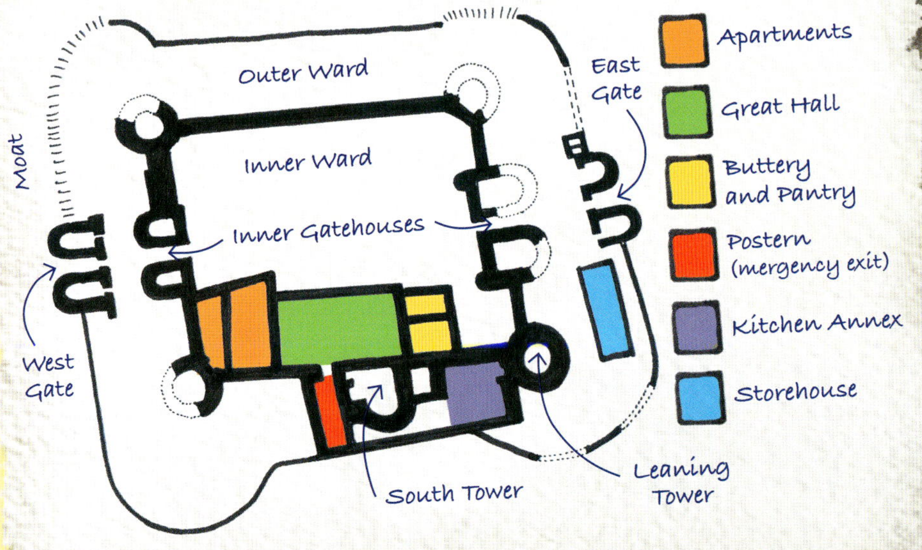

Caerphilly Castle is a concentric design. An outer wall protects the higher inner walls of the castle.

The walls of Morlais Castle lie in ruins but the crypt below is still there.

How do we know?

The centuries after the Norman invasion were a time of great castle-building. Some are still standing like Caerphilly Castle. Others, like Morlais and Castell Nos, are in ruins, but still leave plenty of clues about their past.

Caerphilly Castle covers 12 hectares of the town centre (about the size of 15 football pitches!). A double curtain of thick walls surrounded by a moat prevented attackers from overrunning the castle.

Only part of the south-east tower and the crypt still remain of Morlais Castle. The castle was excavated in 1833 by Lady Charlotte Guest, wife of John Josiah Guest, the Dowlais Iron Master. Thirteenth century coins from the reign of Edward I were discovered.

This engraving by the Bucks Brothers shows the ruins of Morlais Castle in 1741.

There are very few written records about castles from medieval times. The Tudor writer John Leland, who travelled through England and Wales in the 1540s, visited Castle Nos (he called it Castelle Nose!) This is what he said about it: 'Castelle Nose is but a high stony creg in the top of an hille'.

Lady Charlotte Guest translated the Mabinogion, a collection of medieval Welsh myths and legends.

Civil War

"Fire!" The command bellows from beyond the castle walls. The cannon blasts and the daily bombardment continues. Inside the castle, there is no shortage of gunpowder and cannon, and corn and beer for the troops are plentiful. So they fight on even though weeks of battle have left the men war-weary, and the horses hungry and short of hay. But the Roundheads are increasing in number. The King's cause is surely lost. Surrender is just a matter of time.

Raglan Castle appears in the TV series, Merlin, and the Time Bandits film.

Llancaiach Fawr was built in 1530. Today it is a museum.

A Royal Visitor

In 1642 the English Civil War broke out between the Catholic King Charles I and his Parliament. Although the Royalists won a few early battles, by 1645 Oliver Cromwell and his army of Protestant Roundheads were winning many more. The whole of Wales was now under English control as a result of the Acts of Union passed during Tudor times. King Charles decided to travel to Wales to persuade the Welsh to fight for him. On 5th August he met Edward Prichard, the Sheriff of Glamorgan, at his manor at Llancaiach Fawr. At first Prichard offered to support the King. But, like most of the rich landowners in Wales, Prichard was a Protestant. Shortly after the King's visit he changed to the Parliamentarian side.

Siege of Raglan Castle

One of the King's most loyal supporters in the Civil War was the Marquis of Worcester. His castle at Raglan became a garrison for 800 Royalist horse and foot soldiers. But by the summer of 1646 the castle was under siege, bombarded by the Roundhead forces led by Sir Thomas Fairfax. Scores of soldiers were killed or wounded and, after 11 weeks, on 19th August the Marquis was forced to surrender. But the castle remained standing. The Great Tower was so strong that only two of its sides were brought down.

When Raglan Castle fell to the Parliamentarians, Cromwell's men tried to destroy it. But it was so well built, they gave up.

Plan of Raglan Castle

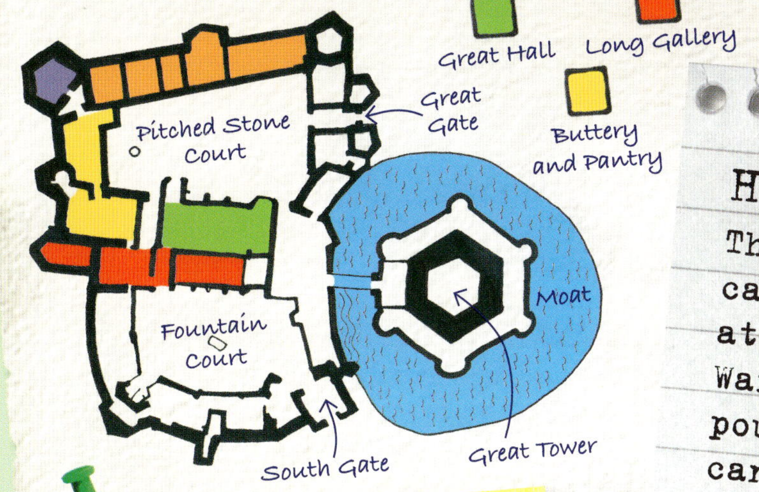

How do we know?

The bottom-half of a two-part cannon shot mould was found at Raglan Castle from the Civil War period. Molten iron was poured into the mould to make cannon balls about 7·5 cm in diameter. The Royalist troops used these in the small mortar cannon mounted on the towers of the castle.

SPOT THIS!

Can you spot this musket that was used in the Civil War against the Royalists?

Hint: look in Llancaiach Fawr Manor.

Iron Masters Rule!

On any other day a cloud of smoke would be curling from the foundry chimneys, the stink of smelting iron filling the air. But today the men in the town are in no mood for work. Shoulder to shoulder they stand, their faces grim and determined. Another band of men marches into sight, their swords shining in the sunlight. A hush descends and Dic Penderyn raises the red flag of revolution. The Iron Masters will not have it all their own way.

The downhill slope of the Glamorgan Canal was so steep that it needed over 50 locks – there were regular traffic jams!

Lock Lewis at Pontypridd was lock number 33 on the Glamorgan Canal.

The Glamorgan Canal

In the middle of the 1700s the sleepy Welsh Valleys changed when wealthy businessmen – the Guests, the Crawshays and the Homfrays – arrived from England. The Iron Masters, as they became known, built great ironworks across the Valleys using the huge amounts of coal and ironstone available underground.

Merthyr became the largest iron producer in the world. Workers came from England, Ireland and rural Wales to work in the new industries. By 1801 its population was more than the totals of Cardiff, Swansea and Newport put together!

The iron was carried by mule and horse-drawn trams to the ports of Cardiff and Barry to be exported. But it was slow work. The solution was to build a waterway for barges to carry the coal. The Glamorgan Canal was completed in 1794 from Merthyr to Cardiff.

The Penydarren Engine

In 1804 a tram road from the Abercynon Basin became the route for the world's first railway steam engine. The Penydarren Engine made its first journey from Penydarren to Abercynon on 21st February. Although the track was only 16 kilometres long the journey still took over four hours to complete!

SPOT THIS!

Can you spot this replica of the Penydarren Engine, built by Richard Trevithick? Hint: walk around the outside of Cyfarthfa Museum.

At Robertstown you can still see the cast iron bridge which carried a tram road over the River Cynon.

Wealth and Poverty

The iron industry made many people in the Valleys wealthy and powerful, but for men and women working at the furnaces life was tough. When profits were low, workers suffered wage cuts or they lost their jobs. To make things worse the Iron Masters paid their workers using their own specially-minted coins known as 'truck'. This 'money' could only be spent in 'truck shops' owned by them. They also made their workers wait for their wages under the 'long pay' system, sometimes for as long as six or seven weeks.

Truck tokens could only be spent in truck shops owned by the Iron Masters.

The Merthyr Rising

The workers started to demand better working conditions. In May 1831 another riot broke out in Merthyr Tydfil. Thousands of angry iron workers marched through the town. Again the Iron Masters called in the army. Soldiers fought with the rioters and several people were killed. One of the leaders was Richard Lewis, better known as Dic Penderyn. He was arrested for stabbing a soldier outside the Castle Inn. The soldier didn't die from his injuries and there was little evidence to convict Dic, but he was sentenced to death anyway. A letter demanding his release was signed by 11,000 people. But he was hanged a few months later in Cardiff.

Angharad Howells is 11 years old and has just lived through the Merthyr Rising of 1831. Unlike many children of her age she goes to school and can read and write well. In this imaginary letter she has a special request for somebody very important in the government in London.

Dear Mr Home Secretary,

I am the niece of Richard Lewis who is also known as Dic Penderyn. I am writing to you to ask you to please have mercy on my uncle who has been arrested and convicted for a crime he did not commit. My Mam says he will be hanged unless you tell the people at the prison not to do it. Mam is my Uncle Dic's older sister and she feels responsible for him. Maybe it was wrong of him to rebel against Mr Crawshay and his men, but he is quick tempered. Anyway you should know how cruelly the people of Merthyr have suffered under the hands of the Iron Masters. Even now they are stopping the men who took part in the riots from going back to work. My Mam says it's like starving them back to work and that people should have the right to protest peacefully. If the Iron Masters hadn't called in the soldiers it wouldn't have all turned out so badly. People have been killed, rioters as well as soldiers. Maybe you don't know that, living hundreds of miles away in London.

I beg you sir, please let my Uncle Dic live.

Your humble servant,

Angharad Howells

Twenty eight men and women were tried for rioting. Some were deported, some punished with hard labour. Only Uncle Dic was hanged.

This plaque commemorating Dic Penderyn can be found at the site of the old Cardiff County Gaol. There is another at the entrance to Cardiff Market.

This is one of two roundhouses that are still standing in Nantyglo, built by the Iron Masters Joseph and Crawshay Bailey.

The iron works in Tondu was built alongside the Llynfi to Porthcawl railway.

How do we know?

Relics of the great iron works can still be found in the Valleys. At Tondu Iron Park, near Bridgend, the original iron works, built in 1838 by Sir Robert Price, have been restored.

The ruins of the Nantyglo Roundhouses are still standing. They were built in about 1816 by the Iron Masters to defend themselves against armed revolt by their workforce. You can see small holes in the door at about knee-height. They are called gun loops.

Newspapers of the time reported the Merthyr Rising in 1831. Read this extract from the Western Mail dated 16th January 1884, and decide for yourself – was Dic Penderyn guilty or innocent?

Under Richard Crawshay (1739-1810) Cyfarthfa became the most important iron works in South Wales. But he was known as 'The Tyrant'.

The troops advanced at the double some miles from Merthyr, and formed in front of the Castle Inn, where they were quickly hemmed in by the crowd. Perceiving this, some soldiers were taken to the windows of the hotel, and the commanding officer gave so many paces to the front and "Order Arms." Down went the muskets on the toes of the mob, and the second rank thus had room to use their guns. "Dick Penderyn" had the reputation of being not at all a bad fellow, and thoroughly courageous. He rushed in, called on all to follow him, wrenched a musket from a soldier, and stabbed him in open fight.

All Work and No Play

Children rush across the road as the school bell rings. Boys toss a rugby ball back and forth; girls huddle together, whispering and giggling. Across the road a hollow-cheeked girl in a thin dress and scuffed shoes stops to watch. Over the sound of the school bell a siren hoots – the call to work at the colliery. The girl bows her head and turns away. No school for her today.

Work or School?

Nearly every town or village in the South Wales coalfield had its own colliery employing hundreds of miners, including women and children. The only education most children had was at the Sunday School, run by the local church. A few villages had day schools attached to the colliery but there were only three in the whole of the Rhondda.

Penygraig Infants School 1907. A little girl in the front row holds up a chalk board with the words 'Class 1'.

Even if their parents could afford to pay the fees, children didn't usually stay in school after the age of 10. By then they were expected to be working, many of them in the coal mines. As a result very few children could read or write, either in Welsh or English. It wasn't until the Factory Extension Act 1867 that children aged between 8 and 13 had to go to school. Even then it was only for 10 hours each week!

The Dowlais Schools

Sir John Guest started the Dowlais Central Schools. He also opened other schools in Pengarnddu and Gellifaelog for his miners' children. A small amount of money was taken from the workers' weekly wages towards the schools' running costs.

Other Iron Masters paid for schools to be built in Georgetown, Pentrebach and Penydarren. But children were still expected to work in the mines and iron foundries.

'Black Diamonds'

Coal, known as 'black diamonds', had been mined in the Valleys since the 14th century. But by the middle of the 1800s, millions of tons of coal were needed to power steam ships and railways. In 1842 the Mines Act made it illegal for all women and girls, and boys below the age of 10, to work underground.

News about the money to be made from 'black diamonds' travelled fast! The largest group of immigrants came from England. By 1861, 18,000 Irish people had moved into South Wales. In Dowlais there were communities of Spaniards too, and in the Rhondda Valley, Italians made a name for themselves, setting up cafes.

The Cyfarthfa locomotive, bought by the Crawshay Brothers in 1897, carried tons of coal.

Between 1850 and 1930 over 3,000 miners lost their lives in South Wales collieries.

SPOT THIS!

The flame of a candle could ignite gases underground, causing explosions. The Davy lamp, which was used underground from about 1815, improved safety. Can you spot one at the Big Pit Museum?

Mining Disasters

The Welsh coal-owners were super-rich men, but for the miners the human cost was high. Underground gases and unsafe working practices made coal mines dangerous places to work. In 1860 an explosion at Risca Blackvein Colliery killed 146 men and boys, and 63 died at Dinas Colliery in 1879.

Josiah Guest is the 11-year-old son of Sir John Guest who paid for the Dowlais Central Schools to be built. Josiah's tutor has asked him to write an account of his visit to the opening of the schools with his grandmother, Lady Charlotte Guest. Here is his imaginary essay.

September 1855

We took the 10 o'clock train from Cardiff and when we arrived in Merthyr, crowds of people stood at the roadside cheering Grandmother. Flowers and flags festooned the streets. As we passed the school in Gellifaelog, fireworks and rockets were set off. It was most exciting!

The shops closed early in Dowlais in preparation for the celebrations. Mr Bruce, the Member of Parliament accompanying us, said that crowds were pouring in on trains and omnibuses from Tredegar, Rhymney, Sirhowy and Beaufort. I had never seen so many people!

At Dowlais House we were seated in the grounds on a grand platform in front of the 1,400 schoolchildren. A marching band played some lively tunes and later a choir sang hymns, then we all joined in with the National Anthem. After Grandmother gave an address we had tea with sandwiches and cakes.

I could not help noticing how small and bent some of the children are. I know that most of them come from poor homes and have to work in my grandfather's coal mines. My tutor says that most working class people are lazy and that it's their own fault, being poor. But I don't think that's right.

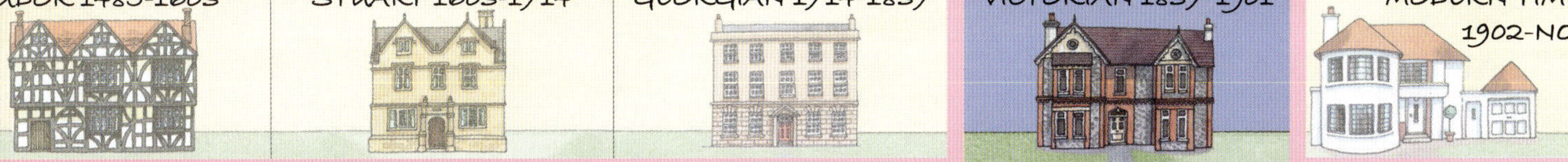

Can you imagine what it would be like to be a child working down a mine?

How do we know?

Child labour in mines like Big Pit was commonplace. In 1842 the Government asked for a report on Children in Coal Mines. This is what they found out: Children as young as five worked 12 hours at a time for only a few pence. Jobs were dangerous and exhausting, loading carts with coal and looking after the pit ponies that pulled them. The mine roofs were low and the working spaces narrow.

This certificate was presented to William Pierce Morgan at the Dowlais Schools in 1868. Does it look like the certificates which are handed out at your school?

Young miners from the Rhondda. How old do you think they are?

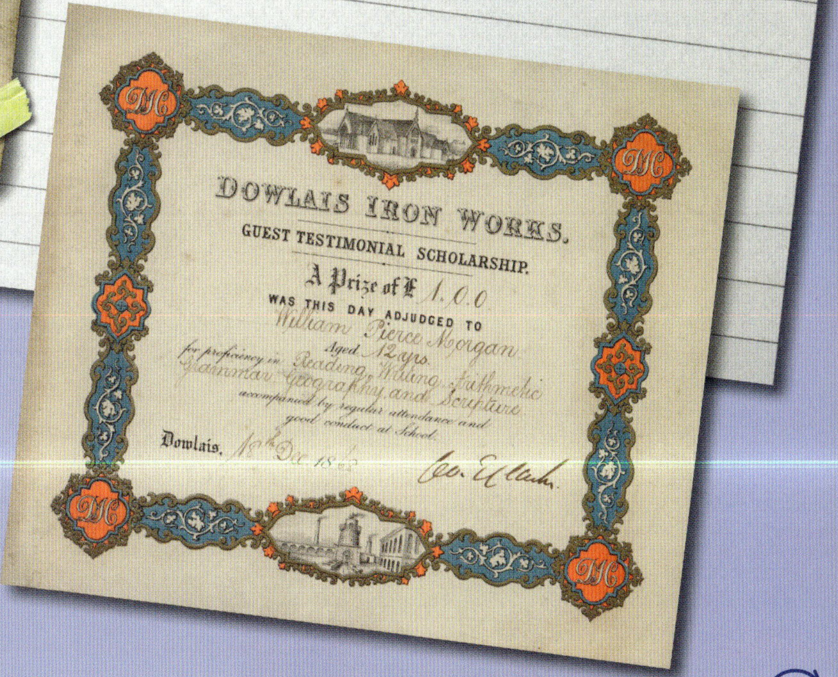

DOWLAIS IRON WORKS.

GUEST TESTIMONIAL SCHOLARSHIP.

A Prize of £ 1.0.0

WAS THIS DAY ADJUDGED TO

William Pierce Morgan

Aged 12yrs.

for proficiency in Reading, Writing, Arithmetic Grammar, Geography and Scripture

accompanied by regular attendance and good conduct at School.

Dowlais,

William Pierce Morgan, 12 years old, was awarded a £1 scholarship for 'proficiency in Reading, Writing, Arithmetic, Grammar, Geography and Scripture'.

Song and Sorrow

The train puffs into the station and comes to a halt with a screech of brakes. On the platform a group has gathered to say their good-byes. The women hug one another blinking back tears. The men's faces are grim. A firm handshake will do. The children skip around the suitcases chanting the word on the luggage labels. *Ca-na-da!*

Trouble in the Coalfield

At the beginning of the 1900s coal mining in the Valleys was booming. Wages had gone up, meaning families could buy better food, clothes and furniture. Some could even afford a holiday at the seaside at Porthcawl and Barry. But when oil began to replace coal and coal became more difficult to mine, demand for Welsh coal fell. One by one collieries closed and miners lost their jobs.

Look at this photo of a family in 1935. Do you think they are rich or poor?

Tonypandy Riots

In 1910 miners in Penygraig went on strike when the pit owners accused them of not working fast enough. When replacement workers were brought in to mine the coal instead, the strike spread. Rioting soon broke out in Tonypandy and the windows of the coal owners' homes were smashed. The situation was thought to be so serious that Winston Churchill, who was Home Secretary, took the unusual action of sending in troops and police from London to control the protestors. Although no shots were fired hundreds of people were injured.

During the riots, one miner died when he was hit over the head with a police truncheon.

The Great Depression

Miners and pit owners continued to clash. When miners were expected to work longer hours for less pay in 1926, they went on strike for seven months. This meant real hardship for them and their families. In Gelli, soup kitchens were set up to provide extra food. In Maerdy, where three of the four pits closed during the 1930s, a rationing system made sure that food was shared out fairly. Many miners who lost their jobs moved away to cities like London and Birmingham where there was more chance of finding work. Thousands of others emigrated to the USA and Canada. This period was known as the Great Depression.

Families picked coal from the slag heaps during the strike.

How do we know?

As pits started closing, thousands of miners went to live abroad. They hoped to find work and a better life. A report from the Times newspaper in October 1907 suggests that emigrating to Canada might have been different from what the miners expected.

Choirs and Chapels

Although there was great hardship Wales became known as 'the land of song'. Chapels organised Gymanfa Ganu festivals. The miners' clubs, like the Parc and Dare, had brass and silver bands. Choirs and bands took part in Eisteddfod competitions. During the Depression the Three Valleys Musical Festival (Taff, Cynon and Rhondda) was set up to try and help mining communities forget the tough times they were going through.

In 1895 the Treorchy Male Voice Choir sang to Queen Victoria at Windsor Castle.

SPOT THIS!

The National Eisteddfod came to Treorchy in 1928. You can still see the Gorsedd standing stones. Can you find them?

Work and War

The young miner blinks as the cage brings his gang back up to the surface. The long shift over, they spill out into the rain, faces and hands as black as the inky late afternoon sky. Soon it will be dark again. *Work in the dark, go home in the dark.* This is a far cry from his job as Accounts Clerk at the council. But someone has to dig the coal while the other men are away at war.

Working for Victory

When World War Two started, men had to leave their homes to fight in the army. By 1943 there were not enough miners to meet the demand for coal. To fill the gap, one in every ten men conscripted to fight was sent to work in the pits. They became known as the Bevin Boys, after Ernest Bevin, Minister for National Service.

Women were also needed to do war work. Thousands were employed in the factories in Hirwaun and Bridgend helping to build aeroplanes, tanks and guns. The work could be dangerous and for many this was the first time they had worked outside the home.

The war brought changes for children too. The government expected that the Germans would drop bombs on London and other large cities. Many families took in children who had been evacuated to safer areas like the Valleys.

Prisoners of War

In Bridgend a Prisoner of War Camp was built at Island Farm. German fighter pilots who were captured in South Wales were kept prisoner there. One night in 1945, 70 of these prisoners escaped through a tunnel. Four of them managed to travel over 160 kilometres before the Austin 10 car they had stolen ran out of petrol and they were recaptured!

Big Pit at Blaenavon closed in 1980. Today it is a mining museum.

After the War

When the war ended some mines and foundries were still working, but coal and iron were less important. Pits in the Valleys continued to close.

Tragedy hit one village in October 1966 when a huge tip of coal waste collapsed on to the village school in Aberfan. One hundred and sixteen children and 28 adults lost their lives.

In 1985, the Government decided to close down the mining industry in South Wales because it wasn't making a profit. Although miners went on strike for a year to try and stop this happening, the closures went ahead. The last pit to be closed by British Coal was Tower Colliery in Hirwaun in 1994.

How do we know?

In 1939 an organization called Mass Observation asked ordinary people to keep diaries recording their everyday lives. The offer was taken up by 480 people who recorded their daily routines, thoughts and feelings. These written records are now kept in an archive.

We also have spoken records telling us about life during the war. Women working in the Royal Ordinance Factory in Bridgend, known as the Arsenal, have been recorded on the BBC History website talking of the dangers of their work.

SPOT THIS!

Every colliery in the Valleys had a rescue team. This rescue helmet, at Big Pit, reminds us of how dangerous the work of the coal miners was.

Bridgend munitions factory employed 32,000 people. Three-quarters of them were women.

The Valleys Today and Tomorrow...

Today the industrial history of the Valleys is remembered through the parks and museums which stand on the sites of the old coal mines and iron works. Big Pit in Blaenavon, the Winding House Museum at New Tredegar, the Rhondda Heritage Park, the South Wales Miners' Museum at Afan Argoed Country Park and the Cefn Coed Colliery Museum are all places where visitors can learn about the past.

A statue to Evan and James James, who wrote the National Anthem, stands in Ynysangharad Park. Will there be a statue to the Lost Prophets in the future?

Tredegar House near Newport was the home of the Morgan family.

The Pontypool and Blaenavon steam railway was built to carry coal in 1866. It is now the highest standard gauge passenger train in Wales.

The Dr Who Studios are in Treforest and many episodes are filmed on location in the Valleys.

Twrch Trwyth was a prince who was turned into a wild boar by a magic curse.

SPOT THIS!

Can you spot this carving of Twrch Trwyth on the forest trail in Cwm Carn? What other carvings can you spot?

Cyfarthfa Castle, once the home of the Crawshay Iron Masters, is now a museum.

Slow down! There's loads to see!

Today Cwm Carn forest trail runs over the old mine workings. Thousands of people visit for the fishing, mountain biking and sculpture trail.

The Parc and Dare Hall was built in 1892 as a Miners' Library and Institute. Today the pits have closed and the Hall is a theatre and cinema. What will it be in another 100 years?

How will they know?

Today's technology may mean that written records are replaced with emails, music, even Facebook postings. Tourists take photos and souvenirs back to their homes for future generations to see. Rubbish tips could give an insight into what people use and throw out. Will things in the Valleys today still be here for decades or centuries to come?

Glossary

AD – a short way of writing the Latin words anno Domini, which mean 'in the year of our Lord', i.e. after the birth of Christ.

Amphitheatre – a round open-air theatre, surrounded by seats which rise from the centre so everyone can see and hear.

Catholic – a member of the Christian religion that considers the Pope to be the head of its Church.

Cavalier – also known as a Royalist: someone who supported Charles I during the English Civil War.

Centurion – an officer in the Roman army, originally in charge of 80 soldiers.

Christian – a member of the Christian religion, which follows the teachings of Christ.

Christianity – the Christian religion, which believes Christ is the son of God.

Cohorts – bands of soldiers in the Roman Legion.

Colliery – another word for coal mine.

Concentric – means having the same centre. Something inside something else.

Crypt – an underground room, often under a castle or church, and sometimes used as a chapel or for burial.

Drawbridge – a bridge that can be raised and lowered.

Emigrate – to leave your own country permanently and settle in another.

Fort – a large, strong building offering support and protection.

Foundry – a place where metal is made.

Groom – someone who cleans and looks after horses.

Kiln – a large oven used for making things such as bricks or pottery.

Legion – a group of between 3,000 to 6,000 soldiers in the Roman army.

Legionaries – the name for soldiers in the Roman Legion.

Medieval – another term for the period of time known as the Middle Ages, roughly from AD 1000 to the 15th century.

Monk – a male member of a religious community that has rules of poverty, chastity and obedience.

Ogham – an ancient alphabet used by the Celts.

Pagan – someone who believes in lots of different gods from the natural world.

Portcullis – a wooden or iron gate, usually in a castle entrance, that can be raised or lowered to keep out enemies.

Protestant – a member of the Christian religion that considers the king or queen to be the head of its church.

Royalist – someone who supports the king or queen.

Roundheads – soldiers who supported Oliver Cromwell and Parliament (the government) during the English Civil War.

Slag heap – where waste from a coal mine is dumped.

Standard – another word for a flag, often placed on the end of a pole and carried into battle.

...1536-1543 Acts of Union, English becomes official language of Wales

Index

Acknowledgements

The author and publishers would like to thank the following people for their generous help:

Kay Kays from the National Museum Wales for all her help; Pontypridd Museum for invaluable research and images; Jeff Thomas for kindly letting us use his castle images; Diane A Walker at Llancaiach Fawr Manor for their photography and images; Scott Reid at Cyfarthfa museum for all his help and advice; the people of St John's Parish Church in Cefn Coed for granting access for photography; Pierre at Tredegar for photographing the tokens; Ceri Thompson at the Big Pit Museum.

The publishers would like to thank the following people and organizations for their permission to reproduce material on the following pages:

Front Cover: Shutterstock/Christopher Dodge; p4, 5, 7: National Museum of Wales; p9: Laura Leahy, www.oldmerthyrtydfil.com; p11: Shutterstock/Marina Kryukova, shutterstock/David Lehner, Colin Smith (www.geograph.org.uk); p13: Jeff Thomas www.castlewales.com; p14: copyright of Llancaiach Fawr Manor; p15: Shutterstock/Lukáš Hejtman, copyright Llancaiach Fawr Manor, Shutterstock/Dee Golden; p16: www.oldmerthyrtydfil.com; p17: Ralph Rawlinson (www.geograph.org.uk), www.Tredegar.co.uk; p18: Simeon Jones; p19: Tondu Ironworks, Sophie Watson Heritage Management Archaeologist Clwyd-Powys Archaeological Trust, National Museum of Wales, Western Mail www.walesonline.co.uk; p20: www.oldukphotos.com; p21: www.oldmerthyrtydfil.com; p22: Shutterstock/ Paul Cowan; p23: Pontypridd Museum, www.oldukphotos.com, Merthyr Tydfil County Borough Council, Central Library; p24: Pontypridd Museum; p25: Pontypridd Museum; p 27: www.bbc.co.uk/wales/history; p28: Shutterstock/Mike Price, Alistair Grieve.

Written by Sue Barrow
Educational consultant: Neil Thompson
Designed by Stephen Prosser

Illustrated by Kate Davies, Peter Kent and Victor McLindon (Advocate-art)
Additional photographs by Alex Long

First published by HOMETOWN WORLD in 2010
Hometown World Ltd
7 Northumberland Buildings
Bath BA1 2JB

www.hometownworld.co.uk

ISBN 978-1-84993-007-9

Printed in China

N
W
E
S
A465
CYFARTHFA CASTLE
Taff Val
MERTHYR TYDFIL
Cynon Valley
ABERDARE
GLAMORG
MOUNTAIN ASH
PARC & DARE HALL
FERNDALE
Llynfi Valley
FERNHILL COLLIERY
Rhondda Valley
MAESTEG TOWN HALL
TONYPANDY
PORTH
MAESTEG
PONT
PONT
Ogmore Valley
TONDU IRONWORKS
M4
BRIDGEND